Damnatio Memoriae

Chai Mahfood

En Route Books & Media, LLC
Saint Louis, MO

⊕ *ENROUTE*
Make the time

En Route Books and Media, LLC
5705 Rhodes Avenue
St. Louis, MO 63109

Contact us at
contactus@enroutebooksandmedia.com

Cover art by Chai Mahfood
Copyright 2024 Chai Mahfood

ISBN: 979-8-88870-303-8
Library of Congress Control Number: 2024952827

Jackson stood outside the cinema with John, adorning a sparkly black corset and fishnet stockings attached to a garter belt. To top off his look, he also wore huge glittering platform heels and a choker with pearls each about the size of a quarter. His makeup was exaggerated and intense, a near mock of the more recent gothic trend.

John chuckled warmly when they walked into the theater, various people dressed similarly to Jackson flooding the room. John looked out of place now, only wearing a casual pair of pants, a button up, and comfortable shoes.

Jackson didn't seem to mind, cuddling up to John when they found their seats and laughing along with other people in the theater. It seemed that he knew them.

When the movie began, John understood the reason for the getup, Jackson's sudden comfortability for PDA, and the reason he looked out of place.

The title and opening introduction played as Richard O'Brien's voice rang out, singing about a science fiction double feature.

Throughout the movie they sang, they danced, they laughed, and they loved. John now knew the character Jackson resembled, Dr Frank-n-Furter. The character was fitting for Jackson to emulate. Presenting himself no longer as the college student

shut-in that John knew, Jackson was now flamboy-
ant, promiscuous, flirting.

The stark contrast that John observed was jar-
ring, and when they left the theater, the persona
didn't turn off, only remaining as they walked to
Jackson's apartment.

In that moment Jackson felt truly at peace, okay
with life, willing to keep living. He didn't know how
being alive felt for so long, and now life was like a
drug he was addicted to, and he never wanted to get
sober.

Jackson woke up on cold concrete, gasping for air as his body ached. His head felt as though it had been run over by a freight train. He ran a hand through his hair only for bits and pieces of dried blood to crumble and fall out. His hand came away with a soft hiss of pain. He looked around where he found himself, an empty lot in the middle of nowhere with sigils carved over his arms and stomach. They bled and stung due to the dirt and gravel caught inside. As Jackson stood up, his legs protested, especially his ankle, which twisted immediately and caused him to collide with the ground harshly.

He groaned as he stood up again, taking the time to balance before he started walking, his eyes accustomed to the dark due to the time spent... Wherever he was—oh, he couldn't remember—it seemed his brain was already blocking out those memories.

Nevertheless, Jackson started walking towards the forest that surrounded him. If he remembered correctly, there was a phone somewhere in a nearby town. He went through that town while on his way to that damned building. Jackson wiped his face and found dried blood around his nose, new blood still flowing down onto his lips. He couldn't have been unconscious for too long if his nose was still bleeding, but with how skewed his sense of time seemed to be, he couldn't be too sure.

He walked for what felt like days before he reached the town. The moon starting to set indicated the time to be around five in the morning. The streets were eerily quiet and empty, adding to Jackson's discomfort. Where he lived, by this time, his upstairs neighbor, Lisa, would be getting ready for work.

When Jackson came across a payphone he almost started to cry from relief, using the quarters he found in his pocket to dial John, who would most likely be awake.

"Hello? This is Father Ward."

"John! Oh, thank God, look—I don't know where I am and... I'm scared. I'm really scared, and hurt, I'm injured, please help me."

"Jackson? What's going on? I thought you were at home. You were supposed to be done on the day Father Garcia reported you missing!"

"What...?"

"It's been three days, Jackson... Where are you?"

"I'm... in a town."

"Do you see any street signs?"

"...Yes - Yes! I see a welcome sign."

"What does it say?"

"I'm in Hartford. Hartford, Connecticut."

"How did you get to Hartford?"

"I don't know!"

"Okay - stay put, I'll be there in an hour."

"An hour?!? How far away am I??"

"Hartford is an hour out of Sterling, so stay put."

"John—wait!"

The line went dead, and Jackson sighed, hitting his head against the phone box, his stomach growling with hunger as he looked around, thirst hitting his body like a truck as he wiped the blood off his face with his shirt. The streetlights allowed him to finally take a good look at himself. He had gone to face Gary with full length jeans and a green SubHumans t-shirt. One of his pants legs was torn off at the knee, turning it into some weird asymmetrical mockery of pants and shorts. The other leg had a rip at his knee, but it was intact. His green shirt now had red stains all over it, and his once yellow shoes were splattered with gore.

Jackson felt as though he looked like some sort of sociopath, covered in gore and viscera as the memories of the cultists came rushing into his head, flooding his senses with what happened. Did he kill them? He did. He remembered. He killed them. Jackson killed them like a man possessed.

His stomach squeezed, and he hardly had enough time to get to an alley before he was spewing the meager contents in his gut all over the pavement, sobbing as he pulled at his shirt, taking deep breaths when he was finally done.

Jackson slid down the wall and breathed. Exhausted doesn't even begin to describe how he felt, how he desired to rest.

He didn't remember falling asleep. All Jackson remembered was that he blinked, and when he opened his eyes he was in the back seat of John's car.

"John...?" Jackson asked, sitting up. "Thank god."

"You almost died in Hartford. How do you almost die in Hartford? Jack you can't pass out in random alleyways. You could've gotten robbed or raped or worse!" John scolded, sighing. "I told Garcia you're okay. The search has been called off, so go back to sleep."

"I'm sorry."

"Don't be sorry, I shouldn't have sent you to Gary."

"John?"

"Yes, Jack?"

"I'd follow you into hell."

"...I wish I'd stop going there."

Jackson chuckled softly before laying back down, slipping into a dreamless sleep.

John shook Jackson awake when they arrived at his house. John was gentle with waking his sleeping body, as gentle as he always was with Jackson. Jackson wondered if the tenderness was due to love, or if this new, more intense tenderness was due to guilt. John had even gotten Jackson Dairy Queen, despite his previous notion that it was 'terribly artificial and disgusting'. Jackson smiled when he saw the bag.

"I figured you'd be hungry." John smiled warmly, helping Jackson out of the car and up to his house. "I thought you'd be taking me to *my* house, John." Jackson chuckled when John blushed and fidgeted. "I... wanted to keep an eye on you. That's all. You've... been through a lot." John said as he opened the door.

John's house was as welcoming as ever, bare bones and simple, yet comforting. There was a worn green couch on the opposite side of the room as the tv and a patterned rug that Jackson had brought back from a trip to Pakistan. Jackson goes every year to visit family. Other than those in terms of decorations the only thing that stood out was the number of crosses in the home. Of course, Jackson had crosses in his own home, but this felt more as a warning to all bad will that John was capable of attack.

Jackson sat down at the dining table and started eating his food, chicken strips and fries, his favorite thing to get from Dairy Queen. Jackson ate slowly, the feeling of fullness in his stomach felt almost orgasmic, something heavenly and divine. When Jackson was done eating, John offered him a shower and a change of clothes.

While in the shower Jackson leaned against the wall, letting the blood in his hair run out and stain the water red. His muscles ached in all the worst ways. Jackson felt like he had already died. A part of him would always stay in that basement, in that building, fighting demons and ghouls. He felt so eerily empty that he wondered if that's what death is, cold, dark, emptiness.

His only comfort was the silence after he stepped out of the shower, a deathlike silence. Jackson looked over his scarred and cut body, at his wrists, littered with old scars that held memories of terror. Jackson hated himself for the urge to do it again.

Jackson needed to hurt physically to take away the hurt psychologically.

But he knew he shouldn't. He couldn't bear to see John's disappointed face. He quickly threw some cold water onto his face (which he found counter-productive, seeing as he just dried his face) and stepped out of the bathroom, going to John's room to find some clothing to borrow.

John had set out a pair of pajama pants and a shirt for him. They were large on him, though, a little too short for him. Jackson wasn't one to complain over the state of clothes that John gave him—John's wardrobe, after all, was made to fit John.

John was sleeping on the couch. The sun was high in the sky, indicating noon. Jackson sighed softly, curling up next to John on the couch and allowing his body the rest it needed.

"I just... I'm sorry, okay?" Jackson muttered, standing out on the balcony of his apartment with a cigarette between his lips. "I'm sorry I'm not good enough for you."

"Jack... I never said that." His sister, Aurora said, touching her hand to his shoulder. Jackson jerked away. "Why even come here?"

"It's mom." She said. "She... isn't well, and she wants to see you."

"Oh really? The same mom who stood by and watched me get beat because you told dad that I pushed you? She wants to see me?!? Wow! Must be

the fucking rapture!" Jackson snapped, lowering his gaze to his trembling sister.

"No- look, Aurora, I'm sorry I snapped." Jackson sighed, taking a drag from his cigarette. "It's not fair of me to keep blaming you, you were six."

Aurora sighed, nodding. "I'm still sorry, but Jack, please. For me, Malaka, and Ihaan." The only three that remained in the house. Jackson hated himself for leaving, but he had to get out.

"Okay... I'll come."

Jackson never thought he'd have to see his sister like that, in a casket, all her joy robbed of her. Jackson opposed the death penalty, always had, but when the man who murdered his sister came taunting him in broad daylight, knowing he couldn't do anything about it, Jackson wanted to strangle him, to watch the light leave his eyes.

Jackson excused himself from the funeral early. He told his sister it wouldn't be easy for people like them where they lived, especially being so close to Blue Ridge, a sundown town.

Aurora liked going for walks. She was only 14, an airhead who died for the crime of losing track of time.

Jackson drank that night; he drank so much he thought he would die.

That day was the worst day of his life.

Jackson gasped as he woke up. He was shaking all over like he had come down with something. His head was pounding, and his vision was blurry. He rubbed his eyes a few times to try to clear them up, finding the blur in his eyes was caused by tears.

It was evening when he woke up, though He must've slept the entire day. John was no longer on the couch. His car was missing, so Jackson assumed he must be out. Letting out a sigh, Jackson relaxed.

"I'm home! Sorry I left!" John called into the house, setting down his jacket and keys. "Jack?" He asked, peeking into his room. He found Jackson curled up in his bed asleep. He had a long couple of days. John smiled softly as he lay down next to him, drifting off as well.

Jackson was recovering from his adventure slowly and surely, but there was always a ghost over his shoulder, reminding him of what he did, reminding him of the lives he took.

The cultists were reported missing. Of course, they were. All that was left of them was a robe and ash, the occasional gore. Jackson got confronted by the police about a rather mangled looking man, but the charges were eventually dropped on grounds of self-defense.

Still, though, Jackson lay awake at night, the demons of his head beckoning him to do something drastic.

To go back.

Jackson wanted nothing more than to forget the ordeal, to abandon the project and go back to his studies as a normal man, but he was craving the rush of adrenaline that came with each fight. More importantly, he craved John's admiration. If he was able to take down Gary and his cult, maybe John would like him more. Maybe John would revere him, even if he failed. Martyrdom didn't seem like such a bad consolation prize.

After his third night of sleepless tossing and turning, Jackson decided to do something about it. His work was not completed. What Jackson was about to do has not been approved by the Vatican, but when had Jackson ever cared for rules?

Jackson grabbed his cross, his rosary, and a pocket knife; after he woke up, he was never able to find his bat, which was rather unfortunate. Either way, Jackson snuck out of his house, traveling down the hallway and into the basement of the complex. It smelled like dryer lint and weed. A lot of hippies lived here, but that's not what Jackson was interested in. He opened a door that not many knew of and went further into the belly of the beast. He had discovered this secret room on a drunken night. A run off connected to the basement, it had stairs leading down just like the main apartment. Jackson remembered tumbling down them and passing out, waking up in a ditch near his apartment. He thought he had dreamed the whole thing, but it was clear he hadn't. With a deep breath, Jackson started making his way down the stairs.

It would've been smarter to take a water bottle, some food, maybe even do this on a night where he was well rested, but Jackson lacked many of these instincts when it came to the idea of adventure. In his sleep deprivation, he might have fallen down the stairs, he might not have. He might have simply zoned out. But he didn't remember the trip down until he was at the bottom of the stairs, sitting on the last step.

He gripped his pocket knife tighter as he stood up and started walking around in the darkness. The wall was cold and damp and dark; it stunk of a place that had not been lived in. His eyes were slowly adjusting, but it was not in any way useful. Jackson stuck his hand out in front of his face, and he couldn't even see it.

Jackson wished he had a flashlight. He felt vulnerable, like a sheep without its dog, a lamb without its shepherd. A hairless bear. A declawed cat.

But petty fear had always had a hold over Jackson's life. He wouldn't let it now, not when John's admiration and love was so enticing that it seemed more necessary than food.

Jackson pressed on, taking his soaked hand from the wall and wiping it on his pants. It felt too thick to be water, but Jackson didn't want to think about what else it could be. He really didn't want to think about it.

Nothing seemed out of the ordinary. The room seemed lighter, but Jackson didn't know if there was a light up ahead or if his eyes were adjusting. The most abnormal thing about all of this was how wet the wall was, which was definitely blood, or Kool-Aid, but if it was Kool-Aid Jackson would think that he stumbled into a Jonestown-style crime scene. He shouldn't joke about that.

It was definitely blood, too thick to be anything else. Jackson wondered how there could be so much blood on a wall, until his hand hit a dry part. Jackson was so surprised he stumbled back, touching his hand to the dry part after recovering from his brief lapse in concentration. It was both rough and worn, similar in texture to those statues people touch for good luck.

The wall gave way when he leaned his head against the block, and Jackson fell through onto the floor, hitting his shoulder at a bad angle and most definitely breaking his nose. God, does he have a habit of falling or something?

He didn't fall far. He could climb back up onto the first level if he wanted to, and he did want to. So, he climbed back up. As he pulled himself onto the floor of the level, he could've sworn something grabbed his leg and tried to drag him back in.

Now the hairs on the back of Jackson's neck stood up fast, a feeling of being watched fell over him, like he was a rabbit and whatever was there was a wolf.

Oh, how Jackson wanted to run, but he couldn't seem to move.

Petrified, Jackson held his breath, hoping that whatever was there wouldn't see him if he didn't move, but he felt hot breath on his neck and that was all it took to break the spell. Jackson ran; he ran faster than he thought possible, getting to the stairs and tripping his way up them. Right as the thing managed to grab his ankle, he kicked the door shut, sending whatever was chasing him tumbling back down.

He breathed heavily, heart pounding. His mouth was dry, and his legs were shaking.

Jackson etched a cross into the door before jogging away.

The first book Jackson remembered never wanting to put down was Frankenstein.

Maybe because of how he related to the creature.

Jackson remembered being called a 'sissy boy' a lot in his childhood. It made sense in his mind; he was a thin kid with long hair and a more androgynous fashion sense.

But it still didn't sit right with him.

The first time he had read Frankenstein he was in middle school; it was for his English class.

The creature's description reminded Jackson of himself—long hair, something ugly.

Jackson refused to call the creature a monster; he was made fun of for this.

Jackson called the creature Adam; he was made fun of for this.

Jackson did anything, and he was scorned.

Jackson felt comradery with the creature, whose sorrow was similar to his own.

Maybe it was because they both were outcasts, with people unwilling to see the goodness in them. They couldn't control the circumstances of their births. If Adam was a victim of circumstance, Jackson would've been the same.

But Jackson could never see himself as more than a perpetrator of violence—he used his words to tear walls, demanding that he have the answers to why he wasn't like the other kids at school.

Jackson shook his head when John requested to see his house. "Oh... no, you wouldn't like it." He chuckled nervously as John raised his eyebrow.

"How so?"

"I haven't cleaned in a while."

"Neither have I."

It seemed the two were now at an impasse, Jackson a rock and John a hard place.

Truth be told, Jackson didn't want John to see his apartment because he didn't want him to see the aftermath of his last episode. He was certain he had hallucinated everything he saw in that basement, but there was still a lingering fear on warm lonely nights that he would turn over in bed to drink a cup of water and someone would be looking through his window.

Jackson was scared to fall asleep, so he would fill his body with caffeine and other stimulants until his body forced him to pass out at odd hours of the day. Whenever Jackson awoke, he would be consumed with a fear that someone had broken in.

The sigils carved into his skin now faded into deep raised scars, noticeable no matter what he wore. The Connecticut summer did nothing to allow him to hide them. He started carving in new wounds over them, hoping people would stop looking at him like he was a cultist and start looking at him like he was a nutcase.

Jackson's house was littered with bloody tissues because of this.

But John couldn't be swayed. Even still, the two did need to do some investigating, Jackson's nightmares made John believe it was some form of divine intervention, leading them to the answer they needed to stop this mad man.

First step was to turn Jackson's home into a sort of safe room. It'd be best to do this at night, despite how badly Jackson wanted to do it in the middle of the day, or not at all. But a cult wouldn't be active in the day, according to John. If they could catch them in the act and stop them, they could banish the leader forever.

Jackson wondered if John needed to have his psychiatrist called on him again. John gets like this sometimes. Delusional is the word the shrink used, 'manic episode' this and 'mental institution' that. Jackson would jump off a roof if he ever got locked in the looney bin again, and John's brain might break if he went back.

Unideal circumstances, naturally.

The two men spent the night purifying and blessing each room in his house. Jackson's anxiety grew worse and worse as the day wore on.

"I don't think this is a good idea," Jackson said eventually as the two took a break to eat a late dinner.

"We have to, Jack." John responded, taking a bite of the microwavable ramen Jackson had prepared. "I don't want to either, you know. It's the lord's will that we do this."

"Well - yeah I know it's just," Jackson let out a sigh as his words tumbled around his brain. "I just don't think it's a good idea, at all. John, we should call the police and not go after them ourselves."

"No." John snapped, standing up and knocking his seat back. "The police are tainted by the devil. Only you and I are pure Jack." John said as he grabbed Jackson's rosary. "We do this because the world is impure."

Jackson was shaking, near tears and frozen in fear. He hardly registered anything John had said, only focusing on the sigils carved into his skin from that night, how badly they hurt now despite being healed. Jackson only remembered the paralyzing fear he experienced that night in that house. Oh, god, he couldn't even look at the color red without feeling like he was being hunted.

Jackson nodded though. "Yeah... purity, got it." He said softly as he put his food in the fridge. "I'll get my cross."

John grabbed Jackson's wrist when he walked by him. "I'm sorry." He said, kissing Jackson's hand. "I got... carried away. The world isn't like that - I didn't mean to say it like that." He sighed. "Go get your cross, Jack, I'll be waiting in the laundry room."

Jackson pocketed a knife.

The two descended down the stairway Jackson had found slowly, John holding a bible and Jackson holding a flashlight and cross. He never told John about the knife. Don't show your defense mechanism if you think someone might harm you.

Jackson knew, logically, John wouldn't hurt him, but there was a lingering fear. John changed when it came to demons and ghosts and spirits. He was no longer sweet and gentle and reassuring—he was brutish.

The two stepped off the staircase as Jackson scanned the room. Huh! The blood was missing and the floor he fell through was fixed. Maybe these were underground units, or a storm shelter, or anything.

But when Jackson looked back for John, John was already gone.

Had John not been there at all? Jackson's brows knitted together in confusion as he took a deep breath. No, no, John probably started walking. Never trust a guy who gets lost in his own house.

He started walking, slow, deliberate steps, trying not to make a sound or put too much weight on the floor in case it fell through again. He looked back and forth constantly, grumbling to himself about how this was how people died in slasher films.

Jackson took his knife out of his pocket and gripped it until his knuckles turned white, finding a room full of closed doors. John must be ahead. Jackson could call out to him at any moment, but he couldn't force his mouth to move. He couldn't force his muscles to move.

When did he get here. In this room. No more doors stood in front of him. Did he just start moving?

He searched the ground for his flashlight, finding it out of battery. God, how long was he down here?

His eyes adjusted well enough to the darkness to get a sense of his surroundings. He was in a room. It was round, and at one end of the room there was a hallway; on the other side there was a horrible smell, like rotting putrefying meat. Jackson gagged and retched before jogging over to the hallway to escape the smell. He didn't want to know what was behind him.

He walked down the hallway. As he walked, he couldn't shake the feeling of being watched. Having a useless flashlight didn't comfort him one bit—only the thought he could use it as a weapon to knock out an attacker came to mind, which made him chuckle slightly. Use a flashlight like a bat, what's next? The rosary as a whip?

The idea was laughable as Jackson continued his search for John, but now he was totally lost, no clue where exactly he was going, or where he would have to go if he was in danger.

Dying didn't seem bad now, surviving did.

Jackson only had one encounter with Gary, and that was enough to remind him what the fear of God felt like. Jackson came across a mirror at the end of the hallway, in between two open doors. He looked into the mirror and stumbled back with a yelp. Something was climbing out of the mirror. Its fingers were sharp, and it smelled like a dead body left to decompose in a fire pit. He shut his eyes tightly and squeezed his body in, praying it wouldn't see him, praying it didn't have eyes, praying it would be a quick death.

After a minute, Jackson opened his eyes again, and it was gone, along with one of the doors.

He stood up slowly, looking back at the mirror, but only now seeing his own face. It was oddly dirty.

Jackson ran into the next room, not wanting to give whatever it was the chance to catch him in the hallway again.

The room wasn't empty per say. Quite the opposite, it resembled a child's room very closely. There were stuffed animals on the bed and books in the corner and a stereo on the desk. There were dolls and toys scattered around the room, a circular rug on top of the carpet, and glow-in-the-dark stars on the ceiling.

It was oddly tranquil, making Jackson wonder if he had stumbled into someone else's house for a minute before his attention was brought to the bed; there was a body under the covers.

Jackson froze, wondering if he could leave without waking up whatever was sleeping, but it was far too late for that. The blankets started to slowly pull themselves back, as if possessed, and that familiar scent of rot hit his nose as the sleeping being sat up. It was demented, an affront to God.

It screeched like a banshee, so loudly the room shook. Jackson in his frenzied and scared brain grabbed his cross, hitting the thing on the head with it to knock it out before hiding under the bed when he heard footsteps.

Oh, why did it have to be red? There was a cloaked figure that walked into the room. Jackson knew it would find him eventually, checking behind the curtains first, then the closet. Jackson's breath hitched in his throat when the figure walked to the bed, lifting up the blankets.

Jackson stabbed him in the eye and ran out, barreling down the hallway so fast his lungs felt like they'd give out. He went through every door he found. Every move he made, he felt like they were gaining on him. They'd catch him eventually.

Jackson turned around quickly in the heat of an encounter, slamming the thing on the head with his crucifix before beating him down with it. Even when it was knocked out, Jackson continued to slam the crucifix against it body until he released the pain that impelled him.

He sat there for a while, frozen, paying no attention to the world around him before finding it within himself to crawl out of his own head.

The body was no longer there, but the blood was.

Jackson stood frozen, tears welling up in his eyes as he left the scene. "John...?" He called as the tears slipped down his face. "John? Where are you?" He asked in a shaky voice. He realized if he wanted to get out of this... corridor without going back into the room he started in, he'd have to go through the closet. Maybe that's how he got in in the first place? Maybe. But Jackson was just a man. If anything, he was closer to a little boy than a man, a shaking, scared little boy who wanted his mom.

With a steadying breath, Jackson went back into the room he had just exited and opened the closet door, revealing a long hallway with a light at the end of it. Oh, he was so happy to find a light.

He ran down the hallway. Maybe John had a pocket flashlight? Maybe John was an angel?

John wasn't there. Jackson found himself in the room the two started in, the lamp attached to the ceiling now on.

The light didn't comfort him. If anything, it made him feel like a target, like the men who held torches on Odysseus' fleet, only to be eaten by Scylla.

Jackson couldn't stay here.

Mind over matter, he started running up the stairs. If he could get to a phone, he could call Father Garcia, and they could find John.

He pushed the door open and collided with the dusty floor of the laundry room, finding John.

John was just standing there, his cassock clean as ever.

"John...?" Jackson mumbled; the priest looked over. "Oh my god!" John rushed over, holding Jackson and helping him up. "What happened to you?"

Jackson couldn't answer; he only cried. "I want my mom!" He yelled between choked sobs; he wanted the feeling of safety. He wanted to go home.

"Shhh... shhh..." John said as he stroked his hair. "John! Where did you go? Why did you go back upstairs?!" Jackson sobbed.

John's face fell.

"Jackson... I never went down there. I was waiting for you."

Jackson gasped awake, tears flowing freely down his cheeks as his mind twisted the events of the attic—of that damned house—into something terrible. His hair was sticky with sweat, his upper lip salty with snot and tears, and he needed a shower terribly bad, fearing he was losing it.

Red. The color of his shampoo bottle was red. The color made him want to scream, to vomit, to plunge a knife deeply into his stomach, to drink, to do a line, to get drugged, to do anything other than sit with that stupid, goddamned terrible horrible no good color. Red. It stung like the fresh cuts of Jackson's arm (What are you supposed to do after a great trauma? Not cut yourself?). It felt like the fear of knowing that someone was around the corner. It was the smell of burning yourself with boiled water while trying to make some noodles for lunch. It was the sound of getting a hit with a firecracker on the fourth of July. It was the taste of expired milk, the feeling of nails on highway rail metal.

Jackson threw his shampoo bottle out of the shower, not caring where it landed as he stared down at his arms. He'd relapsed into cutting himself again, ever since the attic, ever since the encounter, ever since the beginning of the end of his life.

And how did Jesus bear the cross? How did he muster the strength to walk to his own death throughout his life? How did he not break down at the age of twenty six, sobbing as water poured around him, and contemplating just burying his face in the rising water until he passed out?

And how did Mary give birth to her son? Did she know? Did she know her womb was a grave?

And how did Adam continue life after losing his rib, knowing that God penetrated him, and not the dread of knowing he was touched by God, but the dread of knowing it would never happen again. How did he not beg for God to take another, and another, beg to be unmade and remade?

And how did Eve manage to smile after her and Adam's exile, bearing the harshness the earth had to offer after falling for a lie when she didn't know what a lie was? She had no reason not to trust the snake.

Jackson didn't want to think. He didn't want to feel. He didn't want to hear, taste, smell, or touch. He wanted his particles to disband. He wanted to be a spiral, a sequence, a paradox.

There was something at work in Jackson's soul. Deep down, Jackson knew he'd never be the same after the incident. He knew a part of him had died. Did John know what the cultists had done to his body after he fell unconscious? Because he didn't, he didn't know what they had done to him, and that scared him.

He knew they carved into his skin, taking a knife to his flesh like one would with a sacrificial lamb and cutting him open, but did they do anything else? And if they did, how should Jackson go about knowing that they did? Body and bones are easy to heal, but the psyche is much different territory because the mind doesn't adhere to the same logic that the universe does.

Jackson should call John.

He stepped out of the shower, all soggy and tired, all sad and numb. Every single mistake left him a little older, uglier, meaner, smarter in a worse way.

Jackson redressed himself in those stupid shark printed pajama pants John had got him for Christmas one year, along with a white shirt from the first live band he ever saw, back when he was into folksy music.

He dialed John's number, twirling the cord in his index finger as he leaned against the kitchen table, feeling like a teenager again due to the motion.

"John?" Jackson asked when the line picked up. "It's me, Jack."

"Jackson? What's going on? Its three am." John's voice was raspy. Jackson had clearly woken him up. God, he felt bad about that.

"Sorry to wake you," Jackson said. "I just... I had a really bad nightmare—can you—" He sighed, pinching his nose bridge as his lower lip trembled. "Can you come over and keep me company? I'm uh... I'm really scared."

John sighed over the line, exasperated, clearly, but the sound of gathering keys told Jackson he'd be coming.

"I'll be there." John said before the line hung up. Jackson hung up his phone and sat down on the kitchen floor, leaning against the dishwasher.

He felt trapped, the darkness of his home at night consumed him like a migraine pounding on his skull. Jackson wished he had the words to describe how he felt at the moment, but he didn't. There were so many things and thoughts going through his head at this very moment that he couldn't differentiate them from each other, curling up on the floor and covering his ears like a cowering child. His suffering was so profound that he was certain nobody would understand it.

Except Jesus, but then again, did Jesus have sigils carved into his skin? Did Jesus have the fear of not knowing what the cultists did when he had passed out from pain? He was too sore from running to tell what muscles were sore. He was too tired to notice anything when he woke up, dumped in a random alley way like... like his sister was when she was found dead.

John arrived as fast as he could. His knocking startled Jackson so badly he felt like his heart would leap out of his throat, but the knocking came in a pattern so distinctly John that his panic was short-lived.

Opening the door, Jackson knew how bad the scene before John must've looked. The two could survive the trauma, sure, but could they survive the aftermath?

"Jack? What happened?" John asked as the two sat down on the couch with a mug of tea. Jackson sighing as he blew on his beverage.

"I had a nightmare—we were going in the basement—well, we went in the basement, but then you weren't there... I was in a hallway, it was dark. I lost my flashlight. There was a painting—I can't remember what it did or why it scared me, but it did. There was a room, and I hid from... Something under the bed. I bludgeoned it with a crucifix. There was so much blood everywhere."

Jackson took a sip of his tea. The burning of his tongue felt good, a reminder that he was indeed alive, very, very alive.

John sighed, running a hand through his short brown hair. "I brought some oils and holy water; would it make you feel better if I blessed your house?" He asked, meeting Jackson's gaze.

"Yes... yes it would. It would make me feel much better, Father Ward." Jackson responded, putting his head in his hands as John rubbed his back and shoulders, feeling the weeks worth of pressure to service others finally spill out of Jackson in an almost orgasmic release of sorrow, John didn't judge. John didn't speak. He simply sat with the weeping soul and rubbed his back in soothing circles.

Jackson always serviced others. He was the eldest child, the first son. Sure, his sister had it worse, being the eldest daughter, but Jackson was put into the position of the third parent at the age of six. He didn't know then, but he stopped being a child at six, delegated to putting his siblings to sleep and watching them when their parents weren't there taking them to school or helping them with homework.

By the age of twelve, Jackson was officially promoted to the third parent. He was the one to cook for his siblings, change their diapers, feed them, make sure they had everything they needed.

But the issue is, when you spend your whole life servicing others, you forget to service yourself. Jackson grew up under the notion that any form of self care was selfish, that it would lead you down a dangerous road to hedonistic whims. As an anthropology major, Jackson understood now that the concept of hedonism was designed to put shame on things that shouldn't be shameful. Hedonism was made up to place moral value on taking pleasure in sensory experience. Hedonism was created as a way to separate humans from animals, but all the ways that separation was conducted only led to suffering.

Jackson took away one message from his first class, "Pursue what makes you feel good, and practice radical rejection of the constructs meant to turn you into a machine."

And the hardest part of all of this is the feeling of not being fully incarnated. Jackson couldn't grasp the material reality with full intensity. A part of him seemed to reside far away and beyond what's tangible. His reactions with the world happened through a sensorial and emotional bubble wrap; dull, cold, lifeless. He was piloting a marionette, knowing that he should really embody it. The highs and the lows, the joys and the hits—he understood them, but did not absorb them. They don't integrate his being where they should serve for growth.

Experiences seem to go through him instead of staying within; the memories remain but not the meaning. What should have served as the building blocks of a personality had been flushed away: what results is a man who's just as lost as the kid he once was, not in terms of physical necessities, but in the sense of self. No goals, no plan of execution, no drive. Just being.

There's a piece missing or malfunctioning in the mechanism that shapes him as a person. Nature or nurture, body or mind, he doesn't know. He remains a self-aware observer who can act out his experience and suffers from it, as life demands more than just being present.

And then realization hit Jackson like a brick. As John stepped into Jackson's room to bless it, Jackson realized something. He had to return—he had to return to the house where it all started, back to the house—the attic, the basement, all of it.

He would have to return. He had to. His soul was being pulled toward it. Was it a lack of adrenaline? A manic episode? Jackson didn't know.

He came up to John, tapping his shoulder.

"I'm going back," he said. John looked shocked, shaking his head quickly.

"No! No, you aren't, I should have never involved you in this mess with Gary." John grabbed Jackson's shoulders, hugging him tightly.

"Don't go. Don't go back. Don't. You wont make it out this time. I promise they'll kill you. I'll kill you."

But Jackson was willing to knock down heaven's door, hugging John back and burying his head in the crook of his neck, sighing softly.

"I..." Jackson sighed, pulling away from John and meeting his eyes. "Come with me," he said, taking John's wrist. "Come with me," he repeated, pleading, begging.

John looked at Jackson like he was crazy. He didn't want to go back as much as anyone else. He'd had enough from the cult, from the Martin house, from this whole thing. He didn't want to go back. Not in a million years.

But something compelled him. He didn't want to give in. John was a priest, excommunicated, sure, and repenting and paying his penance to be welcomed back into the church, yes, but he was still a priest in Jackson's eyes, and he didn't want to let down such a kind young man.

But did he have the strength to? He didn't know. John was scared, scared of Gary, scared of failing another exorcism, scared of losing Jackson in the same way he'd lost Father Allred.

"...you're sleep deprived." John said. "Go to bed. I'll stay here." He guided Jackson to lay down, letting him smell the oils as he placed them on his wrist, and leaving the room.

Jackson was tired, but the kind of tired that seeps into your very bones—the type of tired that makes you want to simply cease existing. Yet, the kind of tired that makes even suicide seem like a chore. But he fell asleep easily knowing John was in the other room on the couch. He was lucky to have him, count that among his blessings.

Blood and bones were easy to hurt, but a certain bastard had left his behind, his spirit passing on. After everything that man had done, he didn't deserve to die, but Jackson would find him. He'd get his revenge come hell or holy water.

First, Jackson brought some wine to hell, but the devil only grinned and sneered, "That prick isn't here, he's up in the kingdom." A long, sharp nail pointing up as the flames licked at Jackson's skin.

"I'll make you a deal." Jackson said, extending a hand to shake. "I'll do your punishments for you, and you get me up there." He spoke.

The devil grinned, thinking over the deal before shaking Jackson's hand. Jackson got to work pouring bleach in a couple sinners' eyes, and when his task was completed the devil sent him on a bullet train to the Lord with a gift, a polished 1911.

Jackson pushed his way up to the front of the line, demanding to see the big man himself.

And there he was, approximately four-foot-five. "Good to see you, son!" he boomed out.

"You know what he's done." Jackson sneered, aiming his gun.

"Listen, you ain't who I'm looking for, so just step aside or I'll paint these gates crimson." Jackson cocked the gun. "And I know a kingdom without a king is just dumb. Step aside or I'll fill these clouds with blood."

And God said, "No, you're just confused. One day your day will come, but this is just a big mistake..." Jackson stared at him, confused indeed.

Cause when Jackson opened his eyes John was laughing. "You're having one hell of a dream!" He chuckled as Jackson looked around his room, everything as it was, the memory of his dream fading like he'd just gone to confession.

"How do you feel?" John asked, sitting down on the bed as Jackson sat up, rubbing his temples.

"I... better. Yeah. Better." Jackson assured, taking a sip from his water bottle. "I had... a really weird dream."

"Oh?"

"Yeah... I was... I was in hell, then in heaven, and I had a gun." Jackson sighed, running a hand through his hair.

"What time is it?" he asked. John looked down at his watch before responding.

"Ten am." He said, standing up and groaning as his knee protested.

"I'm so sorry Jackson, but I gotta head out." Jackson sighed, nodding, as he hugged John tight, the smell of the oils lingering on his shirt.

"Thank you, Father." He said as John returned the hug, smiling warmly.

"Don't do anything stupid, Jack." He scolded before chuckling, hugging Jackson one more time before leaving.

He left Jackson with his thoughts once again. Jackson never did well with his thoughts. They were one of the few things in life that he had almost no control over. There is a constant stream of thought throughout everyone's heads every day. Being able to control those thoughts would be a miracle, but one can't control those thoughts. (Author's note: if you could, I wouldn't have written a book in the first place, but look where we are.)

So, Jackson instead chose to throw himself into cleaning. Laundry that was long overdue was placed in the washing machine along with his bedsheets. He swept and mopped his floors, vacuumed his carpets, watered his plants, took out his trash—all in attempts to hide from what he was really thinking about.

John.

He loved John, more than any man should love another man. It went beyond friendship, beyond adoration, beyond mere romance, even. Jackson couldn't even begin to explain the feelings he felt when his eyes met John's, overcome by emotion, grief, love, rage, sadness, joy, all muddled up inside of Jackson's disembodied mind.

He knew he'd never be able to share these feelings, not in a million years, not even in either his or John's dreams. Over his dead body would he tell John. He couldn't even risk going to confession because he knew the priests at the church. He couldn't even fathom living that down if it was Father Garcia he confessed to!

So, he'd avoid, and he'd avoid his feelings and avoid everything he thought about and maybe one day he'd meet a nice Catholic girl and they'd get married even if that's not necessarily the life Jackson could envision for himself because every single fantasy of the future he'd always envisioned was one where he was with a man.

And that was terrifying. Jackson already knew he was gay. There was no hiding that, no denying it, but there could be avoidance. There was a pandemic going on in the gay community. Jackson donated blood to those with AIDs. Hell, when this all started Jackson was paranoid because his best friend and first kiss died.

So, avoidance was the way to go. Like with most sins, avoid the way you feel, control your temper, control your language, control your feelings. That's what Jackson was raised to believe.

Jackson finished cleaning at one pm. Hungry for lunch, he pulled on some simple day clothes before venturing out to the bus stop. Once on the bus, he sat and waited for where he got off.

In the corner of his eye, he saw a man in a red hoodie, the hood pulled up over his face, and he was back, back in that house, back with the cultists and the cages, back delivering two of whatever the hell he was delivering into MOLOCHS navel, back to being chased, back to being interrogated, back to the hell he had found himself in because John needed him, and how can you refuse the person who makes you feel corporeal?

He got off the bus early, trying to keep his panic at bay as he walked. His blood sugar needed to be fixed. Instead of going to the Filipino market as he had originally planned, Jackson went into a sandwich shop and ordered something simple, eating quickly before leaving.

The Martin incident was recalled to Jackson's memories as he found himself on a hiking trail. How he got there, he didn't recall, but he was walking, the air fresh and crisp, the smell of pine needles and sap filled his nose as he found a tree to climb.

The Martin incident was something John often used as a sort of warning for Jackson, a cautionary tale of hubris, the cause of his excommunication in the first place. Jackson did not want for his fate to end the same as John's, a sad ex-priest trying so hard to become reinstated. Jackson saw how hard he worked. It was evident when he was placed into the Yale Psychiatric Institute. Jackson visited him every week.

He climbed down from the tree, feet landing on the soft dirt with a thud, reinstating a knee pain he had long since tried to forget about. He must've twisted his knee wrong when he was at the... The house.

He tried to forget about the house.

About the blood, the viscera, the fluids, the squelching of boots against deflated bodies, the crunch of bones, the animosity with which Jackson treated the cultists, banging their heads in with his crucifix—the way they fell limp. Jackson had been acting on impulse, he knew that they had attacked first and had means to kill. Jackson acted in self defense; nobody knew what he did. Nobody.

Yet Jackson does. Jackson recalled exactly what he did, how even when they were laying, shaking and convulsing in pain, Jackson didn't stop. He didn't stop until they stopped moving completely. It was like he was in a trance, and when he awoke from it he was in a parking lot with no sense of what had happened after he passed out from exhaustion.

Jackson had gone to confession and confessed an act of wrath to the priest, but he didn't specify what he did, nor did he specify the events that led to it. He simply informed the priest that he had caused harm out of anger.

It wasn't anger. It was rage, white hot rage boiling over, rage over everything in his life finally popping like a cyst. A red hot cyst, with blue rage, bright blue rage, blue brighter than that of the brightest star.

Jackson had built up his life in an effort to defend, and so he defended himself against those he held close, those he saw as threats, and even himself, and he was very good. Jackson had crafted himself in such a way that nobody would beat him down again. A hand is a hand is a fist. Jackson would not cower like a dog; he would not lay down and accept his beatings.

Jackson would go back to hell.

The Martin house was dim, dust having settled over the furniture and floor. The smell of a house that hadn't been lived in for a long time permeated the air and filled Jackson's nose as he walked. Grabbing out a pen from his pocket, his pen with the built-in flashlight that John had given him after he expressed a fear of the dark.

He didn't have his crucifix with him, nor did he have any form of scripture or holy item with him, but he did have a pen that John had given him, and an unblessed cross necklace, and that felt like enough. If worse comes to worse, he'd use his leather belt to defend himself. That had to work, right?

Jackson's footsteps disturbed the layer of dust on the floor, kicking it up into his eyes and lungs. He coughed, blinking rapidly and praying there was no mold in this house.

He found himself going into the basement, re-calling John informing him of this being the spot in which he'd found Father Allred's dead body, his mouth being puppeteered by Amy in some sick form of ventriloquism. If only Amy wasn't possessed, and it was all a gag, that would've made for a great photo.

The basement consisted of more dust, a broken wooden chair and snapped robes, as well as blood. The putrid smell of rotting meat filled Jackson's senses, and it took him everything he had to not retch and vomit. Covering his nose with his shirt, he con-tinued forward, squinting to see in the dim light.

Blood was on the floor, dried, it seemed, but that didn't explain the rotting meat smell, which Jackson noticed was radiating from a pile of boxes in the cor-ner. Crossing himself and praying for strength, Jack-son reached the boxes, prying them open.

The smell was so powerful that it caused Jackson's eyes to water. He clutched his necklace, pulling away from the boxes as the basement seemed to stretch endlessly, causing him to become increasingly dizzy as he tried to find the stairs again. Something didn't feel right. Not just feel—something was not right. Jackson couldn't figure out what it was, and he couldn't find the stairs.

He searched blindly, the dust filling his eyes and blurring his vision, causing tears to form as a means of getting the foreign object out. His senses were useless. This basement seemed to defy all logic, all sense, as if it was being unmade and remade within a matter of nanoseconds. One moment, Jackson was on the stairs, and the next he was in the corner of the room, still staring down at the boxes, empty, too empty. They appeared endless, and Jackson felt himself compelled to fall inside.

He felt his body tipping inside, and within seconds he was falling, colliding with a wooden floor, like a shed, or a cabin, or the attic.

There was a bed in front of him. It seemed he had fallen just short of it. The sheets were tousled and dusty, like the rest of the house, but Jackson smelled the distinct scent of John's cologne on the sheets. It was faint, but it was there.

This was the Martin House, the location of John's failed exorcism over a year ago.

Jackson took in his surroundings. There was a desk to the left of Jackson. On it was a purple prayer mat, some photos, a clinic pamphlet, and some school notes. Amy wasn't even out of high school when she was possessed. It filled Jackson with a weird sense of catharsis. In the far right corner was a dresser, still filled with clothes, with one drawer slightly ajar. On it was a purple doll. To the left, there was a shelf, filled with books, comic books, choir books, scripture, everything under the sun. To think such a vibrant girl could've been possessed by such a horrible entity! It threatened to make Jackson lower his guard.

A door opened upstairs.

Slowly, Jackson crept out of the room, finding himself in a series of strange connections before spotting a staircase, the door wide open. Cautiously, he followed it up.

The attic had all the signs of John's struggle with Amy—dried blood and viscera, a broken window signifying the way she'd leapt out when John had almost succeeded in saving her, her rotting body still down in the backyard when Jackson poked his head out of the window. Her neck was broken, her face was... gone.

Jackson gasped at the sight of the gaping hole where her face should have been. It wasn't that she had no skin; she had no face. Fearing for his life,

Jackson ran back down the stairs, trying the door only to find it locked. Left with no other choice, Jackson smashed a window open with his boot, shards of glass sticking into his body and causing blood to be drawn.

The pain didn't register in Jackson's mind, too focused on getting away. He ran, and ran, and ran, panting, gulping breaths, sucking air greedily as his jaw and shoulders ached, his legs shaking as he drooled. The feeling of that paralyzing fear didn't let up. Jackson had no clue where he was going, but he knew he had to get out.

Jackson knew that the next thing he did decided which version of himself his loved ones saw again. He crashed through the forest, glass sticking out of his arms and shoe. Tripping and stumbling over rocks and downed trees, he crashed into hikers, a man, woman, and two children.

He didn't know why they screamed at the sight of his face, but he grabbed the man's hand, kneeling, sobbing and pleading with them to get out of the forest. It was haunted by something horrible; it was possessed by an entity; something was coming for him.

Jackson screamed loudly at the sight of a red-robed figure, thrashing away from the family and making a mad dash for it. A few minutes later, he was nowhere to be found.

Jackson's mind was in too many places at once, living a failed exorcism he wasn't present for one second and reliving the horrors he experienced in that house John sent him to the next. He collided with a rock, sending him flying into a bush in front of him, digging the glass further into his wounds.

Now, he registered the pain he was in, looking down at his cut up torso from his escape from the Martin house. No time, this forest was demonic, and if he chose to stay, he'd get swallowed up whole by it. With a limp, he got up and continued walking, focusing on getting out of the forest.

He wondered about the hikers; would they call the authorities? An ambulance? Jackson sighed. He definitely needed an ambulance right now, maybe also some tequila.

Each step taken was painful, sending surges of brilliant white agony through his legs, up to his spine. Looking down and pulling up his pant leg, Jackson revealed why. His knee was absolutely demolished, bloodied and beaten. Hell, Jackson was sure he saw muscle, maybe even bone.

No time for that. He'd stitch it up when he got home. The body'd heal itself. In the back of his mind, he imagined John telling him that that wasn't how the body worked, but he chose to ignore this, leaning against a tree.

Jackson felt like a hostage in his mind. Though, he supposed it was nice to be held.

Sucking in a deep breath, Jackson pushed himself off the tree. He didn't know where he was going, but he knew he had to get out. He walked, waiting for the sound of cars. He knew a highway ran next to this forest. He could hitchhike.

It wasn't until sunset that Jackson finally stumbled out of the forest. By now, he'd gotten the majority of glass out of his skin. He tried to wave down someone, but nobody seemed to want to help a bloodied man. He couldn't blame them. John was reluctant to let him into his car after he got a nail in his foot once, worried about the blood staining the mats.

So, Jackson walked. He knew vaguely the direction he was supposed to go in, but he didn't know exactly how far he should walk before each turn. After all, he didn't have a map on him because why would he have a map on him?

A truck driver, seemingly sent from the lord himself, pulled over, asking Jackson if he was okay. Jackson nodded but requested a ride, the driver was reluctant but agreed, asking where to.

"576 Candleglow." Jackson said, sighing as he eased himself into the seat and tried not to bleed everywhere. Most of his wounds had already coagulated, but some where deep enough to continue to bleed.

Jackson arrived on the street and thanked the driver, walking up it and up a driveway, knocking on the door.

"Father Ward? John! It's me! I need help!" Jackson yelled as he pounded on the wooden door. When John opened it, he looked pale, ushering Jackson inside.

"Oh my gosh what happened to you?!" John yelled, immediately sitting him down at the kitchen table and grabbing a first aid kit.

"I think I need to go to a hospital." Jackson said, groaning in pain as John extracted the remaining glass with tweezers and pressed a wet cloth to the injury. The ex-priest gaped.

"You think?!?" He said, wrapping his wounds in gauze. "I think I'm taking you to a hospital," he said, helping Jackson up and into the car.

"I saw her." Jackson said as they drove. "I saw Amy, she was... She was dead, but she chased me." John sighed, rubbing his nose bridge.

"Yes, she jumped out of a window and... And died on impact when I returned to her home." John confessed solemnly, guilt over the Martins and the unfortunate fate of Amy was a cross John bore, his personal sword of Damocles, the noose wrapped around his neck.

"...She had no face." Jackson said, looking over at John's face, observing the scars near his ears from a close call with Gary. John almost had the same fate.

"Yes." John said. "She... she had lost it."

"It was a portal. It was... She didn't..." Jackson stuttered, trying desperately to make sense of what he saw in that house.

"And the boxes—they were voids. I fell in one and was in her room... I heard a door open... John, I'm not crazy. I swear this happened. I'm not lying. The door was locked. I had to break a window just to get out." Jackson pleaded with John to believe him as he had done so many times before, believe this tale, believe what happened, and help him.

"...Jackson. I don't want you to be a part of this project anymore." John said after a moment, gripping the steering wheel tightly as they arrived at a red light.

"Look at you, I can see your knee cap! You keep arriving at my doorstep in worse and worse shape, sometimes mentally, sometimes physically. I don't believe it is God's will that you are a part of this. You're getting hurt, and I don't want to see that happen. I understand that I was the one to send you to that house in the first place, and for that I do apologize, but I cannot, in good conscience, allow you to continue to involve yourself in these affairs." John spoke passionately, like the preacher he once was. Jackson stared up at him.

"I have to be a part of this," he said.

"No! No! I won't allow it any further! The way to help us right now is to stop getting involved and instead focus on your school work. That's what I need from you now—that's it." John said as they pulled into the hospital parking lot. He helped Jackson out of the car.

"Please. Don't do this. You're going to die doing this." John begged as they entered the building.

Jackson wanted to speak, but this wasn't the time nor place to do so. He was angry. Because if he quits this, then that means all the trauma, all the pain, all the damage wasn't worth something, wasn't for something. It would mean Jackson did all of that for nothing. Jackson wanted his actions to have meaning. For John to essentially deny him that right, the right of meaning, why, it was the most poignant embarrassment Jackson had ever felt.

Jackson was brought back almost immediately, his bone sticking out of his knee and the possibility of internal bleeding, along with head trauma, assisted the triage nurse in getting him his room.

His clothes were cut open so the nurses could get to his injury. Jackson simply stared ahead, trying to dissociate himself from how exposed he felt. The nurses and doctors could see everything, his every scar, self-inflicted or not, especially the sigils, especially his self harm scars. It was more than embarrassing. It was humiliating. Jackson chose avoidance. He'd really liked his shirt, but now it lay in tattered, blood-stained pieces to the sides of him.

Jackson woke up from the surgery on his knee, groggy and high on pain killers. Looking to his side, he saw John sitting next to the bed and praying.

"John...?" Jackson croaked, his voice weak and frail.

John looked up, coming to the side of his bed and sighing, petting Jackson's shoulder-length black hair. "Jack... good morning. How do you feel?"

"Don't make me leave the project..." Jackson begged, holding John's wrist tightly.

"Please don't make me leave... I can be useful, I can help you and Garcia. I can, I promise," Jackson begged. No longer did he feel like a fallen angel, nowadays feeling more akin to a risen demon.

Why don't those exist anyways? If God can forgive anyone, why not a demon? Why not allow them to rise again, to bask in his warm glory once more? Why must they suffer eternal damnation? People change. It's inevitable. Can't the supernatural do that too? The only thing constant in this world was change, so couldn't demons change and rise once more?

John sighed, running a hand over his face. "Jackson, it isn't that simple..." He begged Jackson to yield to the logic of the situation, to see that risking his life on a near-weekly basis was a stupid decision.

"Then... John," Jackson groaned as he sat up, meeting the ex-priest's eyes.

"If you don't let me stay on this project—if you don't let me help you, then all the trauma I endured would have meant nothing. I beg of you, John, let me help." Jackson pleaded, taking John's hands into his own and clasping them together tightly, kissing his knuckles as tears slipped down his cheeks.

"...you don't do anything without me there." John said, hugging Jackson tightly. "No attic, no cults, no sewers, no clinics, no apartments, nothing, nothing involved without me or Father Garcia there to assist you, okay?" John gently wiped Jackson's tears away from his face, before hugging him tightly once more.

"Fine," Jackson agreed, reaching out to shake John's hand. "It's a deal." He laughed as a nurse came in, observing John's clerical collar.

"Excuse me, Father, but visiting hours are over." John nodded.

"I'll be back in the morning, Jack." He said, grabbing his coat and heading out of the room, leaving Jackson once more with his own thoughts.

The sound of the heart monitor beeping was the only thing alerting Jackson to the fact he was still living. He was in pain. The morphine was wearing of. But pain is how we know we're still alive, right?

He pulled back the sheets, staring at his bandaged and swollen knee. God, it hurt so much just to lay down. Jackson couldn't imagine the fun he'd have trying to go to the bathroom.

The hospital room was bare bones as anything, lilac walls and posters, a window to the left of the bed, monitors and wires across the floor. It was clean. It smelled clean, too clean.

Jackson hated the smell of sterility, but supposed it was a good sign for the room to smell as much like rubbing alcohol as it did. In a perfect world, all odor removers would have been scentless, same with toothpaste.

God, Jackson hoped that should John bring him anything from home he would bring the grape-tasting kid's toothpaste he uses and not the junk-mint flavored toothpaste. That stuff never fails to make him cry.

He stared out the window, slowly standing up with a loud groan and leaning against his IV drip stand to shuffle over to it. Pulling the curtains aside and admiring the stars, Jackson was jealous of them up there in the firmament, the brightness and vastness of it all. There was a certain allure the stars had, as if each twinkle was God blinking one of His many eyes.

Jackson wanted the freedom a star had, to wander around the endless expanse of the cosmos with no repercussions, nothing holding him back, nothing to be tied down to. Jackson was so tired of being constrained to this one place; in fact, nowadays he felt like he'd never get out of the hole he found himself in. Yet, he had made his bed, and now it was time to lie in it.

He was bored. Unfortunately, he had no books with him to read, and as for reading material, all he did have was pregnancy pamphlets, a newspaper on news he didn't care about, and a bible. Suppose he could read the bible. Jackson was a much bigger fan of the Old Testament than of the New Testament. He had no clue as to why. Maybe the drama of it all. Jackson lived for drama, for the heights of human emotion, and the lows of human despair.

Jackson slowly climbed back into bed, careful not to agitate his knee as he pulled the blankets over him. Without his weighted blanket, Jackson felt significantly colder, and much less comforted, like a shaved bear.

The setting of the hospital room reminded Jackson of when he was in the Yale Psychiatric Institution, a place he had just recently learned was the same institution in which John had been held after his failed exorcism, even at the same time.

Jackson was often held in solitary confinement for being prone to outbursts, screaming at any doctor or nurse that dared try to restrain him, sneaking markers onto his person before he was sent into the same padded room he'd been sent to a thousand times, drawing on the pads of the walls and floors. He got his medication dosages upped many times because of those drawings, before he was too high on antipsychotics and muscle relaxants to think.

People who hadn't been to an institution might think Jackson's recollection and description of the institution is stereotypical and barbaric, but this simply was how they were, grooming and coercing the patients into acting in ways the staff deemed "normal." But what is normal? Jackson couldn't tell you. All he could say was that this was not it. For him, at least, hospital trips due to adrenaline induced ever manic satanic panic might be normal for someone else far, far away.

It was unfortunate, but it was true, no getting around it.

A nurse came in to give Jackson another morphine dose. Jackson looked over at him, his expression tired and dazed.

"Got any books?"

The nurse looked down at Jackson, chuckling warmly.

"Go to sleep, Mr. Agbayani. Your body needs to rest and heal," he said.

"Can't sleep. Any books?"

"…I'll check and see if I can sneak some comics for you from the children's ward," he chuckled. Jackson grabbed his wrist.

"You don't think I'm crazy, right?" He begged to know. The nurse put a hand on his chin.

"…I wasn't there when you were brought in," he said, "but from what the doctors told me, you were babbling like a lunatic. Something about a cult of the second death, and a faceless girl, and God not watching."

"Yes?"

"No, the chances of you having a concussion are pretty great. I assume you're disoriented." The nurse said, backing away from Jackson before leaving the room.

Jackson sighed as he was once again alone with his thoughts, turning over with a groan and using a spare pillow to prop up his injured knee. He was tired now that he thought about it. Very, very tired.

The issue he faced now was that he survived the house, but would he survive the aftermath?

Jackson was discharged from the hospital three weeks later, after fighting off a slight infection and healing from his injury, using a cane to get around on bad days for his pain, going to physical therapy to get better, and generally sulking.

The issue with his and John's deal is that Jackson would, indeed, follow John into hell, but before, Jackson was bearing responsibility for John's actions. Now, John would bear responsibility for Jackson's as well.

The idea of someone he held so dearly being brought back to a place so terrible because of Jackson's decision made him feel sick. More importantly, Jackson couldn't run away now like he used to be able to. Maybe he should get his cane blessed, carve some crosses into it while he's at it, maybe make a shoulder strap to store it on his body whenever he wasn't in pain. Would make a good window breaker, too, so that was something.

John and Jackson sat in Father Garcia's house. Fr. Garcia was an older priest with a rather rough attitude, and tons of skeletons in the closet. He was a Mexican immigrant with a mustache that Jackson always wondered how he kept so clean.

"Hijo," Garcia started, sitting next to Jackson with a glass of water in his hand. "What's wrong?"

Jackson was startled at the sound of Garcia's voice, jumping and nearly smacking his hand off his body before he realized who exactly was speaking to him. Then, he visibly relaxed.

"Dealing with a cult is a lot easier when midterms aren't also around the corner..." Jackson groaned, rubbing his temples before taking the water with a grateful nod.

"Thank you, Father."

"I assume John has informed you of my reluctance to have you a part of this project?" Garcia asked as John flitted about the kitchen. Jackson leaned over and nodded.

"He did. When I was recovering from my surgery."

"And I hear you two agreed upon my ultimatum?"

"Yeah, I can't go to any locations without you or him with me to back me up. Y'all are responsible for my actions now." Jackson sighed, taking a sip to quench his thirst.

"Mm. Maybe that'll keep you from these suicide missions you seem to impose on yourself." Father Garcia spoke, his voice steady and deep, raspy in the ways that told you he was a smoker.

"Maybe." Jackson agreed, putting his head in his hands. "I just... I just don't understand why..."

"Why the cult is willing to kill?"

"Yes!" Jackson yelled, slapping his hands on his knees.

"I mean—I'm a jackass but I don't physically torture people, I mean—do you know what they did to

Amy? She had no face!" Jackson was distressed at the memories of Amy's gaping hole in her head, at such memories appearing in his head like a bad omen. Jackson wondered if that would happen to him if he kept involving himself.

Logically, Jackson did want to stop his involvement. Putting one's life in danger by simply going outside is not a smart decision, but Jackson made a deal with a glowing entity.

Maybe he accidentally made a deal with the devil. The devil and his consorts masquerade as God and his Angels far too often.

Jackson might've signed his soul away in exchange for an escape, and that escape might only be temporary while whatever it was made plans for something far more dangerous and far more sinister.

Jackson had beaten Gary for now, but could he keep him beaten? Would he get swallowed up by his acolytes.

"Father—" Jackson started, turning to face Father Garcia.

"Father, I have something to confess," he said, clasping his hands together.

"When John asked me to go investigate that daycare," Jackson couldn't escape what the building truly was, even if in his mind he chose to call it anything but. "I... I was stuck with a needle by a man in a robe. I can't remember... What happened next, it was like I was watching myself in third person. I..." Jackson shuddered.

"I killed them," he admitted, staring into Garcia's eyes.

"I killed them. Like animals. The men, and the women, I slaughtered them like animals. I beat them over the head with my bat—I strangled them with my rosary, I..." Jackson sobbed. "I'm a murderer."

Garcia's lips tightened, eyes widening as he broke eye contact with Jackson, mind whirring to think of a response to this confession. Could he forgive a sin so grave? Jackson hadn't even been questioned. When police came knocking on his door, he lied through his teeth, lied like a dog.

How are you supposed to react when someone confesses murder to you?

"And you were stuck with a needle?" Garcia finally spoke. Rationalize. Detach. "You were out of control of your own body; God will forgive you." But Jackson broke one of the ten commandments.

"God... will forgive you." Garcia said, standing up and leaving the room. Garcia also had a fair share of blood on his own hands. Michael Davies was one of his lowest moments, a 14-year-old boy possessed and kept chained to a bed during Garcia's attempts to exorcise him. He couldn't save him before he got run over by a car.

But this was different. Jackson had committed mass murder, slaughtering any red-robed figure he came into contact with in a frenzy of divine-induced mania. God would forgive him, sure, but would Garcia? Would Garcia look at him differently?

Did John know that Jackson was a murderer? Would John look at him differently? Would John be afraid of Jackson, a man he holds so close to shield him from the monsters of the world? How would John react upon finding out that he was holding the monster all along?

This was a tough pill to swallow.

Jackson stared at the doorway before sighing and standing up, he had to tell John what happened in that daycare, no more sugar coating the truth, no more hiding.

"Father Ward?" Jackson asked as he entered Father Garcia's guest room.

The story came tumbling out of Jackson like food poisoning—the bloodshed, the puzzles, MOLOCH, the encounter with Gary, all of it. John couldn't believe what he was hearing. Mouth agape, he stared up at Jackson, features contorting into horror the more and more the story unloaded.

When Jackson finally finished talking, John was silent, staring with wide eyes at the young man in front of him.

"Say something..." Jackson begged.

"Scream—"

"Yell—"

"Hit me—"

"Please—"

Jackson begged, falling to his knees, palms pressed against each other so tightly they turned white, praying for forgiveness.

John sat silently, too shocked to learn that maybe he was protecting the world from Jackson.

Or, maybe, it was divine retribution for those cultists, those sinners, perhaps they deserved it—no, no, that's a terrible thing to think.

But maybe they did. Maybe they got what was coming to them. Maybe they should've thought twice before their acts of heresy.

Or maybe Jackson was a murderer, and there was no justification.

John would try to rationalize.

"Self defense," he'd say, his voice shaking like a leaf in the wind.

"It was self defense—you were in danger; it was all self defense," John begged, hoping if he said it enough it would be true.

Jackson kneeled silently, grabbing John's knees and sobbing for forgiveness. All the pain he'd suffered through in that daycare came tumbling out like an avalanche. He was not God's strongest soldier.

Jackson had survived the event, but he was certain he'd never survive the aftermath.

He fell upon John's feet, begging to fall upon mercy, and accepted the blame.

After the daycare, Jackson found himself thinking he was dead so often that he felt hands wrapping around his head, sending him down a dangerous spiral, threatening to result in the relapse of some bad habits.

Jackson didn't know how to communicate how sorry he was. His mind was stuck in a different realm. He needed space that people wouldn't give him. He lost his sense of self, looking to the stars for answers but finding those stars black and cold.

"Jackson..." John mumbled. "I... left some papers in my office... May you get them?" He asked gently, petting Jackson's hair and lifting his face to meet his eyes.

"Sweet lamb..." He said, as Jackson sobbed harder.

"I'll – I'll do it – okay..." Jackson mumbled as John pressed a gentle kiss to the crown of his head.

Jackson took a deep breath, grabbed John's car keys, and left the house, informing Garcia of where he was going. Father Garcia suggested they watch a movie when he got back to get their minds off things.

The hairs on the back of the neck serve a purpose, a purpose of protection, a purpose of insulation.

A sign of being watched was the hairs on the back of your neck standing up.

Jackson didn't know why he was so scared. By all accounts, this was perfectly normal. He had been inside this church thousands of times, and he had never felt this scared. John had just forgotten some papers inside his office. That's all Jackson needed to get, so why did he feel like he would vomit if he stepped in further? Why did Jackson want to flee from somewhere he always viewed as safe?

This was the same church he always went to. It was the only church in the area that had a Tagalog service. It was John's church. It was comfortable and safe. The gold trim of the walls was the same, and the stained glass windows and the painted tapestries were the same, but something felt so wrong about the church at this very moment. No longer could it protect Jackson from whatever horrors awaited him when he left. God was not watching.

He forced himself to move. The sooner he got the papers, the sooner he could go back to John's house. And the sooner he got back to John's house, the sooner they could resume their movie marathon. It was difficult, but Jackson forced down his anxiety along with the bile in his throat. The office was the same—the same leather rolling chair and desk, the same wallpaper and bookshelf, the same decorations and red pencil holder.

Red. Why did the color red make Jackson sweat, as if the very color would open a portal to hell, as if the color would reach out with a trident and stab him, as if the color would carve sigils into his unconscious body, as if the color would chase him through a corridor, screaming, slashing claws chasing him as he ran and ran and ran—

Jackson froze when he heard footsteps, a sob rising in his throat as he willed himself to turn around. Sweat dripped down from his neck to his chest, staining the green shirt he wore alongside his fear.

But nobody was there.

He rushed into John's car, breathing in and out as he put the key into the ignition, his fingers trembling as he pressed down on the gas. The red rosary John kept in his car was mocking the young devotee.

He pulled into an empty alley, staring at the rosary before grabbing it with shaking hands. Even though he wasn't in the church, he couldn't shake the feeling that he was being watched, or was it that something was no longer watching. He couldn't tell.

He was vulnerable as his heart beat like a drum. The color red, once a color he loved, taunted him, daring to show its ugly face as he spit on the rosary and chucked it into the back seat. Gripping the steering wheel tightly, he drove back to Garcia's house to deliver John his scriptures.

Or was it that he was still in the psych ward, and he was hallucinating it all.

Or was it that he was still in the house, forever fighting for his life against an army of unyielding, untiring, enemies, covered in red, the red of his own angry wounds, the blood of the bludgeoning he had done. The miniature bible felt heavy in his pocket as he tried to focus on the movies, catching the last bus to his apartment after their marathon of picture shows, the memory of their laughter keeping him warm on this cold night. Connecticut was unforgiving in her winters.

He sat still on the bus, the blue seats familiar to Jackson, stains of mysterious origin and sticky floors like a shitty college bar, leaning against the glass of the window as the bus started on its route back to Jackson's apartment. In the reflection, there was a man in a red hoodie.

Red. Red always made Jackson sweat, feel like he was on an edge of a cliff with his feet in cement, feel like his life was one he had to run from. The mere color feels like a threat, a sign of doom.

He turned to the hooded man, but there was no one across from him. He was going insane, wasn't he? He was losing his mind, surely. Maybe he should consider checking himself into a psychiatric ward, of his own free will this time, instead of the last time when he had the cops on him during a suicide attempt.

Perhaps he was losing it he figured as he looked back to the window. His reflection seemed to lag a little, but he couldn't tell if that was because of the movement of the vehicle or a trick of the eye due to the dark environment. The feeling of uneasiness did not abate though, not since he visited the church. He could dull it, fill his life and thoughts with something to forget about it for a while, but when he was alone it crept into his thoughts, filling his blood with the need to run away and not stop running until he reached some place he could call home. Back in Appalachia, back in the Philippines, back in Pakistan, maybe. Maybe.

Maybe Jackson could simply accept this as the new normal. It could always be worse.

No. No not actually. It could be worse, sure, but how many other college students have to live in an apartment run by a cult? At least the rent is low. Jackson made sure of that by shooting a gunshot into the sky every month.

He trudged to Father Garcia's bathroom to shower before the movie marathon, looking at himself for a while before undressing to shower. God knew he needed a shower. His messy black hair filled the webbing of his fingers as he bathed before he sat down in the soapy tub and let the water beat down on his head.

Red. Father Garcia's shampoo bottle was red. The minimal tranquility he had was interrupted as he grabbed the bottle and threw it out of the tub, angry tears welling in his eyes as he curled up on himself tighter.

The color red could fly, yet had no wings, speak without vocal chords, slither like a snake or walk like a dog. Sometimes, it moved like and mimicked the people he knew, making him second guess his own sanity until he was stuck in a padded room. The color red was solitary and company, corporeal yet incorporeal, always moving like a river and yet dammed. Under his nose and over his head, it was out of reach.

Jackson didn't find any of this funny, but the voices of the past filled his ears. Jackson had known the fear of God.

And he also knew God wasn't watching.

He felt like something had crawled into his belly and taken up residence, syphoning off his own life like a parasite. Or a baby. He felt the tendrils of darkness and fear, the red tendrils reaching into his mouth and planting their young inside of him.

And he hated that feeling, the feeling of being used, the feeling of being forced, the lack of free will.

The scars on his body are a grim reminder of how he was treated when he had fallen unconscious, the sigils carved into him, the violation he felt when he woke up bleeding and bruised, a sacrifice.

The mirror's reflection lagged.

It wasn't even trying to pretend to mimic Jackson.

It just stood there. Smiling.

Jackson knew it wanted out.

He left the bathroom quickly, heart beating like a drum as he entered the living room.

He couldn't even focus on the movie. He wanted his mom, to curl up once again in her womb, safe from the world. He wanted to move back to his childhood house. He'd promise he'd be quiet. It would be just to sleep.

Jackson craved the comfort his mother had once provided him, even if it was bad, even if she was bad. Because he knew the sacrifice she had made to bring him into the world, foregoing medical school for the sake of raising Jackson.

And he would beg to know why he wasn't good enough for her to truly know him. She loved him sure, but Jackson didn't think his mom liked him as a person. If they hadn't been related, it's likely that they would've never been friends.

Jackson had fallen in love with a war that had been long-ended. It ended when his mother finally died and his youngest brother was sent to live with an aunt and the house was given to his younger sister to inherit when she turned 18. Aurora would've turned 18 this year.

When the movie ended, John went to the guest room, Garcia went to his room, and Jackson set himself up on the couch, his mind replaying the events of the day.

He missed who he was greatly, before the daycare, before the cult—just a damn good kid trying his best, not a career workhorse or force of ambition, just a useless ray of goddamn sunshine.

Jackson scribbled out a note for John and Garcia to read in the morning. Throwing on his coat and stealing one of Garcia's crucifixes, Jackson left the house.

John found the note before Garcia, panicking as he woke up the older priest.

I'll be gone by the time you two read this, I've snuck out enough to know how to leave without waking anyone up.

This note is likely the last time you'll hear from me. I've gone to confront my personal demons, not Gary, not the cult. I'm confronting myself.

I probably won't survive it, and if this night was the last we see each other, I just want to say thank you.

You two gave my life a purpose, even if it was for a little while. I understand that what I am doing is selfish. I was given a gift of life, and I'm essentially throwing it away now, but that's for God to judge me on.

If I don't return, I've placed my coordinates on the back of this note. Come find me if I'm not back within a week.

All my love, Jackson Agbayani

P.s, John, I should let you know this. It would be selfish not to tell you. Mahal kita, John, higit pa sa pagmamahal ng isang lalaki sa ibang lalaki.

Jackson stood in front of an old church. The church had been the cause of six children's disappearance in the 60s, and Jackson knew the order of the second death would be hiding out here.

What Jackson was about to do had not been approved by the Vatican.

And God is not watching.